Use these holiday stickers to make gifts for your cool friends!

HARPER
An Imprint of HarperCollinsPublishers

Use these holiday stickers to make gifts for your cool friends!

HARPER
An Imprint of HarperCollins Publishers

As Cool As It Gets

Written by **Jory John** • Cover illustration by **Pete Oswald**

Interior illustrations by **Saba Joshaghani** based on artwork by Pete Oswald

HARPER

An Imprint of HarperCollinsPublishers

The Cool Bean Presents: As Cool as It Gets

Text copyright © 2022 by Jory John

Illustrations copyright © 2022 by Pete Oswald

www.harpercollinschildrens.com

ISBN 978-0-06-304542-2

The artist used pencil sketches scanned and painted in Adobe Photoshop to create the digital illustrations for this book.

22 23 24 25 26 PC 10 9 8 7 6 5 4 3 2 1

❖

First Edition

WATCH OUT! Here come the holidays!
Bells are ringing. Jingles are jingling.
Tinsel is . . . tingling?

Whump!

Whatever. It doesn't matter. The truth is, I don't usually feel very festive, jolly, or merry this time of year.

I may be a cool bean . . . but I don't always have the coolest holiday season.

Oh no.
No, no, no.

Here's why: every year, there's
a big ol', fancy ol' holiday party.
All the beans in town are there
to celebrate and whoop it up.

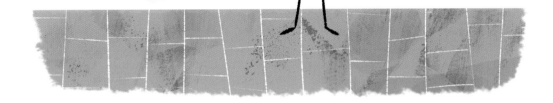

And every single year, we have a gift exchange.

To enter, you select a bean's name out of a hat. This year, I randomly picked Beanadette J. (Not to be confused with Beanadette S.)

Beanadette J. is one of the coolest of the cool beans and I knew she would be expecting one of the coolest of the cool gifts.

It's kind of a big deal.
There's a lot of pressure to be a great gift giver during the holidays.
After all, what's cooler than making someone's day with an amazingly expensive present? Am I right?

Of course I couldn't buy her something
extravagant like that.
I had no bean-bucks to my name!

So I tried *finding* a gift for Beanadette.
I went on a treasure hunt across town.

Alas, all I found was an acorn,

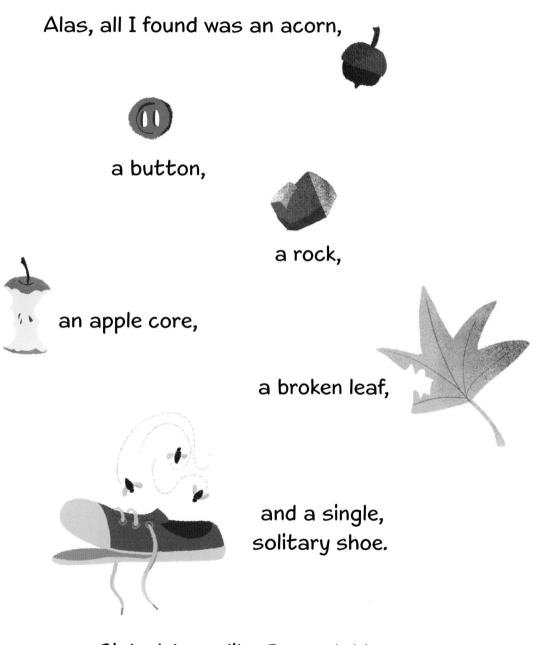

a button,

a rock,

an apple core,

a broken leaf,

and a single,
solitary shoe.

Sigh. A bean like Beanadette
wouldn't want *any* of that stuff.

I considered not going to the party at all. I could hide in my house with the lights out, in case anybody came looking for me. Things would be easier that way.

But then, just as I was starting to panic, I spied some pens and paints and paper in a dusty, forgotten cabinet.

"Hmm," I hmm'd. Suddenly I had a cool idea!

It had been a while since I'd done anything creative,
but I decided to give it a whirl.

I drew a line. Then another. Then another. It started out as a
simple landscape. Then I added a couple tigers . . . a lightning bolt . . .
a sporty car . . . an electric guitar . . . and a double rainbow! I topped
it off with a sketch of Beanadette herself, looking oh-so-very-cool.

After an hour or two, I admired my illustration. It had humor. It had heart. It had a lightning bolt. Was it the best thing I'd ever made? Perhaps.

TO BEANADETTE

I put the drawing in a folder and headed to the party before I could talk myself out of it.

It felt like a long walk.
By the time I arrived at
the house, I'd started
having second thoughts.

This was *before* I saw the gifts
stacked in the corner, stretching
all the way to the ceiling.

And then I remembered my silly little folder, containing a silly little drawing.

Oh no.

No, no, no.

I sheepishly placed my gift on the stack, not making eye contact with anybody.

HAPPY HOLIDAYS

HAPPY HOLIDAYS

HAPPY HOLIDAYS

YAY HAPPY HOLIDAYS

Finally, a bean named Charlene dinged a glass.
"It's gift time!" she hollered. "Gather 'round!"
All the beans sat in a circle. A few friends waved me over.

"YEAH, THIS SHOULD BE REALLY FUN!"
I said, way too loudly.

Then I laughed
awkwardly.

Ummm . . .
ha ha ha?

Haaaachooo!

Then I sneezed on somebody's plate of cookies.

Yow!

Then I bumped my knee on the coffee table.

Everybody just stared.

I spotted Beanadette sitting straight across from me, looking excited.

"Sorry in advance," I thought.

All the beans exchanged gifts. Immediately there were yelps of approval. It was a cavalcade of shiny, expensive stuff, like . . .

electronics,

clothes,

jewelry,

you name it.

Finally, it was my turn. Oh, the dread! But there was no way out.
"Let's get this over with," I thought.

Beanadette took the folder and shook it, listening for a rattle.

She smelled it, in case it was sweet.

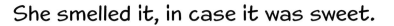

Finally, she opened it and gently removed my artwork, holding it in both hands.

She stared at it for a full minute. There was only silence.

"I knew it," I thought. "The worst gift of the party.
Time to disappear forever."

I started plotting my escape. Just as I was about to sprint to the door and never look back and start a new life somewhere, Beanadette finally spoke up.

"WAIT . . . YOU DREW THIS FOR ME?"
she asked.

"Um . . . yes," I said,
feeling a bit queasy.

"Goodness! This is the absolute COOLEST present
I've ever received," she said.
"It .... is?" I asked.

"It's totally and
completely . . . wonderful!"
she said. "This gift is as
cool as it gets!"

Everybody crowded around my drawing.
All the beans had nice things to say about it,
like, "Wow!" and "Neat!" and "Cool!"

What a feeling!

Whew!

I'd created something unique and original. I'd given it
away. And it had made somebody happy.
All in a day.

The rest of the party sped by in a blur of
holiday music, sweets, and fun games.
Some of the other beans asked if I would
make drawings for *them*.

Oh, and I *received* a neat present, too! It was a scarf that a bean named Gene had knitted for me. He'd been really nervous about *my* reaction, he said.

I told Gene how much it meant that he'd taken the time to *make* me something.

And my new scarf kept me cozy when I went outside.
It was truly a cool—and also *warm*—gift, indeed.

The walk felt shorter this time.
I had pep in my step and a smile on my face.

So yeah, this has actually turned into a pretty cool holiday season, after all.

I've realized that a gift is a gift, whether it's bought, found, or created from scratch.

I even came up with a new motto:

"When in doubt, just *make* something."

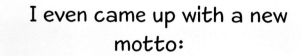

So that's what I'm going to do from now on.